Meet Croa

Kraaaark!

And the crazy Roman family he lives with.

Jeremy Strong once worked in a bakery, putting the jam into three thousand doughnuts every night. Now he puts the jam in stories instead, which he finds much more exciting. At the age of three, he fell out of a first-floor bedroom window and landed on his head. His mother says that this damaged him for the rest of his life and refuses to take any responsibility. He loves writing stories because he says it is 'the only time you alone have complete control and can make anything happen'. His ambition is to make you laugh (or at least snuffle). Jeremy Strong lives near Bath with his wife, Gillie, three cats and a flying cow.

www.jeremystrong.co.uk

ARE YOU FEELING SILLY ENOUGH TO READ MORE?

THE BEAK SPEAKS
BEWARE! KILLER TOMATOES
CHICKEN SCHOOL
DINOSAUR POX
GIANT JIM AND THE HURRICANE
KRAZY KOW SAVES THE WORLD – WELL, ALMOST
THERE'S A PHARAOH IN OUR BATH!

JEREMY STRONG'S LAUGH-YOUR-SOCKS-OFF JOKE BOOK
JEREMY STRONG'S LAUGH-YOUR-SOCKS-OFF EVEN MORE JOKE BOOK

The Hundred-Mile-An-Hour Dog series
THE HUNDRED-MILE-AN-HOUR DOG
CHRISTMAS CHAOS FOR THE HUNDRED-MILE-AN-HOUR DOG
LOST! THE HUNDRED-MILE-AN-HOUR DOG
THE HUNDRED-MILE-AN-HOUR DOG GOES FOR GOLD

My Brother's Famous Bottom series
MY BROTHER'S FAMOUS BOTTOM
MY BROTHER'S HOT CROSS BOTTOM
MY BROTHER'S FAMOUS BOTTOM GETS PINCHED
MY BROTHER'S FAMOUS BOTTOM GOES CAMPING

THE KING OF COMEDY

Jeremy STRONG

ROMANS on the RAMPAGE!

Illustrated by Rowan Clifford

PUFFIN

PUFFIN BOOKS

UK | USA | Canada | Ireland | Australia
India | New Zealand | South Africa

Puffin Books is part of the Penguin Random House group of companies
whose addresses can be found at global.penguinrandomhouse.com.

puffinbooks.com

First published 2015
001

Text copyright © Jeremy Strong, 2015
Illustrations copyright © Rowan Clifford, 2015

The moral right of the author and illustrator has been asserted

Set in Baskerville MT
Printed in Great Britain by Clays Ltd, St Ives plc

A CIP catalogue record for this book is available from the British Library

ISBN: 978–0–141–35771–3

www.greenpenguin.co.uk

MIX
Paper from
responsible sources
FSC® C018179

Penguin Random House is committed to a
sustainable future for our business, our readers
and our planet. This book is made from Forest
Stewardship Council® certified paper.

I offer up this work to my Latin master
who, fifty years ago, marked my Latin exam and
gave me minus ten marks out of fifty. Not surprisingly,
I gave up Latin immediately afterwards.
Pace, *Mr Latin-Master?*

Contents

1. Am I Brainy? Yes, I Am!

I just love chariot race days. The NOISE! The
EXCITEMENT! The sheer heart-banging
THRILL of it all! I want to be one of those
chariot racehorses, thundering round the bends,
eyes blazing, mane on fire, hooves pounding like
crazy. Yeah, I want to be a charioteer's horse. I'm
fed up with flapping. I want four long-striding
legs, not flippy-flappy wings.

Whaddya mean, am I a bird?
Do I look like an elephant?
A squeaky squirrel? I don't
think so. I'm a raven. Got that?
A resplendent raven. Corvus,
to be exact. *Corvus maximus
intelligentissimus*. That's me! Go on,
give us a biscuit! **Kraarrk!**

Whaddya mean, you didn't know ravens could talk? Are you mad? Where have you been? Obviously not to school because if you had you'd know that ravens are super-intelligent, which is precisely what *maximus intelligentissimussimus* means. It's Latin and it means 'a very smart bird with a brain the size of the Colosseum'. A raven mate of mine – now he *is* bright – he can count up to sixteen. That's almost a hundred.

And don't ask me why it's called Latin either because I have no idea. After all, the French speak French, the English speak English, the Germans speak German and the Romans speak – Roman? No! They call it Latin. Get over it!

Anyhow, let me put you in the picture. We are at the Circus and, before you ask if there are any elephants or clowns, the answer is a big 'NO!' We are talking about the one and only Circus Maximus here in Rome and it's chariot race day. Or to put it another way it's **CHARIOT RACE DAY, WAHEY!!** In other words, excitement abounds. Can't you hear the noise? The yelling crowds? The blaring trumpets? The dreadful groans when some poor charioteer gets shipwrecked?

Whaddya mean, why are they racing ships? Of course they're not racing ships. It's an expression – an expression the Romans use: shipwrecked. It means a chariot has just crashed, smashed to smithereens and its rider has been hurled to the dusty ground, quite possibly in front of three other charging chariots, not to mention all the horses and pounding hooves. Urgh – makes me shudder just thinking about it. Get the picture? Good. Stop asking questions and just let me tell you, right?

We're all here, the whole family – Krysis (Dad), Flavia (Mum), Hysteria (daughter) and Perilus (son) – and we've come to see our hero,

3

Scorcha. He is the greatest young charioteer ever, except Scorcha has a big problem, namely, he doesn't have a chariot. Why not? you might ask, but please don't interrupt me again. Thank you. I shall continue. *Ahem, ahem.* (That's me clearing my throat because there's some explaining to do.)

I look after this kid, Perilus, right? Nice kid, floppy brown hair, hazel eyes, a few spots and a lot of attitude, but generally OK. He says I'm his pet, but am I kept on a chain like a dog? No. Am I shut in a cage? No. I can go wherever I like, whenever I like, whereas HE has to ask his mum or dad for permission to leave the house or walk down the street. So who's the pet, eh? Toasted togas! He even tells his mum and dad when he's going for a wump. That's what you, being a human, call 'going to the loo'. For us ravens it's having a wump. Unlike you humans, we do all that business stuff in one go, so to speak. Bet you didn't know that. See? You're going to learn a lot from me. I am not called *Corvus maximus intelligentissimussimussimuss* for nothing. (It's difficult to get your beak round that word sometimes.) Perilus usually calls me Croakbag for short, which is not very nice, but he is only eleven.

So I am Perilus's pet, he says, and he's teaching me how to speak. Ha ha! What a laugh. I was speaking Latin years before he was even born!

Now then, where was I? Oh yes. *Ahem, ahem.*
So poor young Scorcha is without a chariot and
why is that? I hear you ask. It's because Jellus
is jealous. Jealous by name, Jellus by nature.
Kraaarrk! (Raven joke. If you don't get it, it's
because you're human. Sad but true.)

Jellus is captain of the Green Team. In chariot
racing there are four teams, right? Greens,
Whites, Reds and Blues. The Greens are the best.
Oh yes! Come on, the Greens! Jellus chooses
the riders for the Greens and he's got his eye
on Scorcha. Scorcha's young, Scorcha's eager,
Scorcha's good! He's also rather handsome in
a Roman kind of way; that is to say he has a
large conk. Oh yes, Rome is famous for its noses.
Flavia and her daughter Hysteria like Scorcha,
especially Hysteria. I might even go so far as to
say Hysteria, who is fourteen, has a crush on
him. Young love, eh? Everyone give a big sigh –
ahhhhh!

The problem is Jellus is getting on a bit. He's
at least forty and that's OLD for a charioteer.
By that age, most charioteers have either retired
or been run over by another chariot. Jellus
shouldn't be racing. He's too old and too fat and
that means he's heavy and that means he slows
the horses down and that means HE COMES
LAST! Like he did today. I bet Scorcha would

7

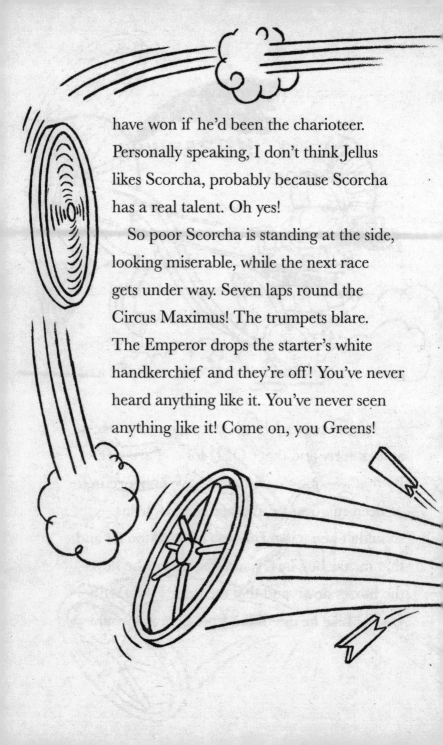

have won if he'd been the charioteer.
Personally speaking, I don't think Jellus
likes Scorcha, probably because Scorcha
has a real talent. Oh yes!

So poor Scorcha is standing at the side,
looking miserable, while the next race
gets under way. Seven laps round the
Circus Maximus! The trumpets blare.
The Emperor drops the starter's white
handkerchief and they're off! You've never
heard anything like it. You've never seen
anything like it! Come on, you Greens!

The crowd yells! 'OOOOOH!
AAAAH! OOOHHH!'
**KRACKETTY – KRRASHHH!
SHIPWRECK!**
The Whites' chariot tried to force the
Reds' off the track at the bend. That's where
all the best action happens. Those bends are
DANGEROUS. The Whites' went thundering
into the Reds' and BOTH chariots have
collapsed, losing their wheels. Well done, Whites,
you've knocked yourself out of the competition!

Numbskulls! The riders have jumped clear, cutting the reins so they don't get dragged after the horses which have gone cantering off by themselves.

Daft beasts, horses, if you ask me. Now they're shaking their heads at each other as if they're saying, 'What am I doing? What are you doing? I'm doing what you're doing and you're doing what I'm doing. We're DOING! Oh, where's everyone gone? Hello? Anyone there?' Hopeless creatures. Get over it!

Still, the riders seem to be OK except for the one being carried off with a broken leg. He doesn't look very happy, but at least he'll live to race another day. (Sometimes they don't!) And guess which team won? The Greens? Of course not. And you know why, don't you? One day, Jellus, you're going to have to let young Scorcha show what he can do because, if you don't, I shall personally fly down and peck your knees until they're right down by your ankles. Hurr hurr! **Kraaaarkk!** Give us a biscuit!

2. Nasty Neighbours

We walked back to the villa very slowly because
we were all in mourning for the Greens, not to
mention Scorcha. Well, the family walked while I
hopped, strutted, flapped and generally made my
annoyance with Jellus clear to everyone. Perilus's
dad, Krysis, kept shooing me out of the way
with his foot so I took a quick sideways swipe at
his left big toe with my beak. I have to say that,
as honkers go, my beak is a whopper, so Krysis
leaped into the air, clutching his foot, and then
had to hop the rest of the way home too.

'Oops, so sorry,' I said. 'I was sure that was
a dead mouse I was peckin'.'

'It was my toe, you idiot!' Krysis roared.

'As I was sayin', Krysis, I am most apologetic.
I could not be more remorseful if I'd actually

eaten your toe. May Jupiter, God of Gods,
rain blessin's, and a plaster, upon your pink
appendage.'

I hope, dear reader, that you are as impressed by my little speech as I was. I must say that, considering I'm a raven, I do have a way with words, thanks to my teacher, Thesaurus.

Perilus was certainly amused. He was grinning at me and pretending to hop and clutch his foot too. Good thing his dad couldn't see him. But let us move on. (Or hop on, in Krysis's case. Hurr hurr hurr! I crack myself up sometimes.)

By the time we reached the villa, Hysteria was in tears, poor girl. She has a habit of bursting into wild sobbing from time to time.

'Poor Scorcha! I really feel for him, Mater!'

(*Mater* – that's your actual Latin again. It means 'mother', in case you didn't know. Aren't you learning a lot? Yes, you are. Here you go, have a biscuit!)

'I know, darling,' said Flavia as she went upstairs. She's a marvel, that woman. I have never seen anyone glide about the way Flavia does. She is tall, elegant and serene and when she moves you can't see her legs doing anything at all. It's as if she's on little wheels. She's never flustered either. Krysis doesn't know how lucky he is to have a wife like that. I'd marry her myself if she was a raven. Maybe I could stick wings on her and pretend. No, you're right, it wouldn't work, would it?

'I'm going upstairs to change,' Flavia told everyone. 'The air at the races was so clogged with dust I could barely breathe. I'll be down soon.' And off she glid. Glidded? Glided? I shall have to check that one with Thesaurus.

Meanwhile, Hysteria carried on bewailing Scorcha being left out of the team. Perilus watched his sister somewhat scornfully. He came across to where I had perched myself beside the pool in the atrium. (Latin – *atrium* – small courtyard; every villa has one.)

'Why do girls make such a fuss about everything?' he asked.

I cocked my head on one side and held his

gaze. 'Why do boys like showin' off?' I asked in return.

Perilus shrugged, so I told him. 'It's to get attention. Hysteria wails. You go tightrope walkin' on our neighbour's washin' line. People pay attention and you're both happy. QED.' (That's proper Latin that is – QED. It means *quod erat demonstrandum*, which is Latin for 'That *maximus intelligentissimus* raven Croakbag has just proved what he said is TRUE and it cannot be argued with.' OK, so it might not mean it in exactly those words, but it means it in spirit.) See, like I said, us ravens are clever. Croakbag? I don't think so. Hey, Perilus! Croakbag yourself!

Kraaarrk!

Perilus sighed. 'You like trying to be clever, don't you, Croakbag?'

'I don't have to try, Perilus. I AM clever. *Corvus brainus giganticus. Toc-toc-toc!*'

'Well, I'm going across to see Scorcha,' my boy announced.

15

Krysis, who was busily winding a long bit of bandage round his left big toe, straightened up and glared at his son. 'Don't spend all day over there with that lad. He might be a fine would-be charioteer, but he's still an ex-slave. You should spend more time with boys of your own social class.'

Perilus reddened. 'Actually, Pater, I'm going to be a charioteer too.'

(*Pater*. Can you guess what that means? You know what *mater* is, after all. Exactly, well done! *Pater* means 'father'. Aren't we getting along well? Have another biscuit!)

Now it was Krysis who turned red. 'You are NOT going to be a charioteer! That is the most ridiculous thing I've ever heard. When you finish school, you will come and work in my office alongside me.'

You should have seen Perilus's eyes. GLOWING. That's what they were doing. Glowing like red-hot coals. 'I would rather BE a slave than work in your stuffy old office!' he yelled and stormed off across the road.

My goodness, the boy does live dangerously, speaking to his old *pater* like that. But then that's Perilus for you. He's a real daredevil. Did I mention his tightrope walking? I think I did, but here's the story.

On the other side of the road from our villa is another big house which is full of tenants. There's Trendia, the seamstress, and her lodger, Scorcha, and the inventor, Maddasbananus.

I'll tell you about all of them later. In particular, and never to be forgotten or taken lightly, are Crabbus and his wife,

Septicaemia. They are the WORST neighbours
ever and I wouldn't wish them on anybody. It's
no wonder Perilus and I call them The Ghastlies.
They are always complaining and making life
difficult for everyone, especially the other people

who share the house with them.

So, the story. One day Septicaemia has been doing her washing, or rather her slave, Putuponn, has been doing the washing and she hangs it out to dry on a rope stretched from The Ghastlies' balcony across to Trendia's balcony. It's the washing line that everyone uses.

Perilus is over there visiting Scorcha, who is teaching chariot-racing tactics to the young lad. Scorcha is telling Perilus how important a good sense of balance is when you're being rattled about in a lightweight chariot. Perilus, being the daredevil he is, tells Scorcha that he has the most brilliant sense of balance already and he will prove it right in front of Scorcha's eyes.

Next thing, Perilus has climbed up to Trendia's balcony and is stepping out on to the washing line, arms outstretched on either side, wobbling about all over the place! Can you believe it? Perilus actually manages to get about halfway along the washing line before the rope breaks!

Down comes Perilus, engulfed in Septicaemia's washing, and thrashes about all over the dusty yard.

Septicaemia comes bursting out of the house like a giant cold sore and starts screaming at Perilus without a thought for

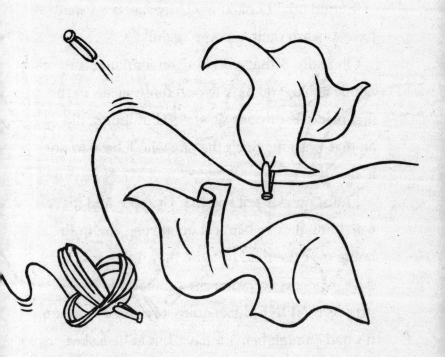

whether or not the boy was hurt.

'You stupid, stupid,
stupid, stupid,
stupid . . .'

Yes, all right,
Septicaemia,
I think we've
got that bit.

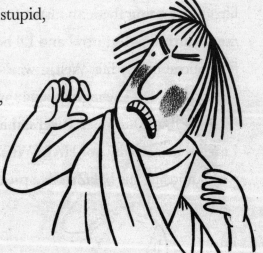

'Stupid boy! Look at my filthy sheets – I shall have to wash them all over again!'

Oh really, is that so? Hang on a minute. Septicaemia, you didn't wash those sheets in the first place. Your poor slave girl, Putuponn, did all that washing. She's the one who'll have to do it again.

I must quickly tell you that Crabbus and his wife think they're better than anyone else in the house over the road because they do have ONE slave, whereas everyone else on that side of the street has NONE. I feel quite sorry for Putuponn. It's bad enough being a slave, but to be a slave to The Ghastlies? I think I'd rather eat slugs all my life. (Slugs being the least tasty of creatures. Give me a bit of dead squirrel and I'll be your friend for the rest of my life. Well, a week at any rate.)

Anyhow, that's what happened with the washing line. Daredevil Perilus, that's my boy. I mean, he actually got HALFWAY ACROSS without losing his balance. He probably would

have made it the whole way if the line hadn't
broken.

And so there we have it. Perilus wants to be
a charioteer, just like Scorcha, who has yet to
become one himself. Hysteria wants Scorcha
to fall in love with her. Krysis wants his son to
follow in his footsteps and have an office job.
And I, *Corvus maximus intelligentissimussimuss*, would
like another biscuit. Thank you very much.
Kraaaaarrrkkk!

3. The Kiss That Changed the World

It was pretty quiet after that for a while, apart from the noise of Septicaemia screeching at Putuponn and telling the poor girl to get a move on or the sheets would still be wet that night.

Whaddya mean, so what? You don't understand, do you? Septicaemia and Crabbus have only got one set of bed sheets because, like everyone else on that side of the street, they're poor. They only managed to get a slave girl because she came cheap (the poor girl is boss-eyed). The Ghastlies don't even pay her. They just feed her scraps and make her sleep with the dog. That's Rome for you.

Like I said, things were quiet so I decided to hop across and go and see my pal the inventor, Maddasbananus. He's completely bonkers, in a nice way. He made me this 'thing' with an oil lamp. It's like a carousel and the heat from the lamp makes it rotate, and hanging from the carousel are little metal cloud shapes. When you light the lamp, the clouds go round and round and they throw big cloudy-shaped shadows on the walls of the room. It's the sort of thing you might give to a little baby, not a bloomin' great big, grown-up, black-as-soot raven.

'I made it to help you feel as if you're out in the open air, beneath the sky and the stars,' Maddasbananus explained.

'That's lovely and you are most kind,' I answered and gave a little bow of thanks and clacked my beak. *Toc-toc-toc*.

The cloud-carousel is very nice and I didn't have the heart to point out to Maddasbananus that (a) although I'm very clever, I can't light oil lamps because I don't have opposable thumbs. I have non-opposable wings, which are only good for flapping about so I would have to get someone else to light the carousel for me. And (b), when it gets dark, I don't light oil lamps anyway – I stick my head under one wing and go to sleep. Last but not least, (c) shadowy dark clouds usually mean it's going to rain, in which case I'd rather be indoors in a warm, dry villa listening to Perilus snoring. (I know, sad, isn't it? He's only eleven and he snores.) But that's Maddasbananus for you: helpful, kind – and bonkers.

Anyhow, he's been inventing again. He keeps making all this stuff. You've never seen anything like it. He's grinning from ear to ear, so obviously he is VERY pleased with himself.

'I'm going to make a fortune from my latest invention, Croakbag,' he said breathlessly. Mind you, he told me that last week with the other thing he invented. What did he call it? A tele-something. Tele-phone! That was it!

'You can use this to talk to people even when they're somewhere else,' he told me.

'Like when they're in the bath?' I suggested.

'No, no, no, much further away than that. For example, if I was here and you were in Pompeii, I could talk to you.'

'What? With that thing?'

Maddasbananus grinned and held it up. It was a curvy sort of object and Maddasbananus held it to one side of his head. The top bit was right by his ear and the bottom bit curved round to his mouth.

'You speak into this bit and you hear out of this bit,' he explained.

'Right,' I said. 'But how does that work?'

'Well, you have to have two of these. I have one and you're in Pompeii and

you have one. I speak into my bit and you can hear me in Pompeii. You speak into your bit and I can hear you back in Rome.'

I shook my head several times. 'No. It won't work,' I told him.

'Why not?'

I held out my wings. 'Can't hold it, can I? And if I held it with my beak I wouldn't be able to say anything. *Ergo*, it won't work.' (*Ergo*; that's another bit of your actual Latin and it means 'therefore'. So now you know.) 'Anyway,' I went on, 'how can I possibly hear you if you're in Rome?'

'Because it's a telephone. That's what the telephone does.'

'All right, you show me. Go to the end of the street with this tele-phone thing and talk to me.'

'I can't do that yet.' Maddasbananus frowned. 'For a start, I've only made one and you need two for it to work – one for me and one for you. Also there are bits missing and I don't know what

they are because I haven't invented them yet,
and thirdly there needs to be some kind of power
source to make it all work.'

'A power source?' I repeated. The only power
source I could think of was a donkey. We use a lot
of donkeys in Rome, mostly for pulling carts and
carrying stuff, so I was having difficulty picturing
how that would work. 'You'd have to connect this
thing to a donkey?'

Maddasbananus was staring at his invention
with that faraway, dreamy, inventor's kind of
stare that inventors get when they're inventing.
At least Maddasbananus does.

'Connect,' he repeated several times. 'That's
the word, Croakbag. Yes, I have to connect it to
something I haven't invented yet and put in the
missing bits that I haven't invented either, and
when I've finished all that it will work. It will
take the world by storm. One day everybody
will have a telephone. I shall probably become a
millionaire. But first I need a bit of money to get

supplies. I don't suppose you've got some you can lend me?'

'You seem to have forgotten somethin', Maddasbananus.'

'Really? What's that?'

'I'm a raven and ravens don't have pockets. Therefore, no money.'

Maddasbananus gave me a wistful smile and patted my head. 'You, my friend, are much more than a raven.'

'Really?' My mind was boggling. What did

that mean, MORE than a raven? What is more than a raven? Did he mean something bigger?

'You mean I'm a buzzard? An eagle?'

But Maddasbananus was back in his inventing world and he drifted off, muttering to himself. 'Connect. Only connect. Donkey, telephone – connect.'

But that was last week and he seemed to have already forgotten about it all because now he was full of his latest and greatest invention – a weaving machine.

'It's a lifesaver!' yelled the great inventor. 'It's going to make me into a millionaire!'

Now where did I hear that before? Oh yes – the tele-phone. And before that the tree.

Whaddya mean, you can't invent the tree? Actually, you're right. You can't. Have a biscuit. You can't invent the tree and that is exactly what I told him.

'They already exist,' I pointed out.

'Not this kind of tree,' said Maddasbananus,

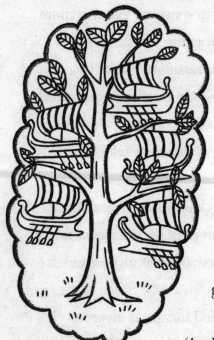

waving his arms about. 'This tree grows something, but not apples, not figs, not oranges. It grows ships. People won't have to make ships any more because my tree will simply grow them.'

'Fantastic,' I nodded. 'And how will your tree do that?'

'Because that's what it does. It's a ship-tree.'

'Yeah, OK, but just callin' it a ship-tree doesn't mean the tree will do it.'

'No? Really?'

I shook my beak and

he went off to think of something else. Anyhow, back to the weaving machine.

Maddasbananus had dragged along a large wooden box with a lid on the top and a door at one end.

'This,' he declared, 'is the world's first weaving machine.' He came up close and whispered to me. 'I have made it for Trendia who is not only beautiful and a brilliant dressmaker, but also the most wonderful woman in the world. When she sees this, she will fall in love with me and ask me to marry her.'

'I think you're supposed to ask her,' I pointed out.

'That's sexist,' said the inventor. 'The point is, this machine will help her with her dressmaking. She will think it's so wonderful she'll fall in love with me.'

'I do hope so,' I murmured. And I really did too. I'm very fond of Maddasbananus and he deserves to be with someone as good and kind as Trendia. After all, in a funny, fashion-y kind of way, she's an inventor too. However, now was not the time for Maddasbananus to go barging in on Trendia because, behind Maddasbananus's back, I could see something I didn't think my friend would want to see.

'I don't think you should go over there just yet,' I suggested.

'Oh? Why not?' And he turned round to look.

NO! NO! DON'T LOOK! SHUT YOUR EYES, MADDASBANANUS! DON'T LOOK!

Too late. As the inventor turned towards Trendia's little apartment he saw her put her hands on Scorcha's shoulders, lift up her face and kiss him.

TRENDIA KISSED SCORCHA! NOOOOOOOOOOOOOOOOOOO!!!!!!!

4. Oh Dear!

Trendia, you're not supposed to do that! Poor
Maddasbananus. He turned as white as a toga.
(Obviously a white toga, not a purple one like the
Emperor's.)

'Ooops,' I muttered. I know, silly really,
but what else could I say? I felt so sorry for
Maddasbananus. What was Trendia doing? I
mean – kissing Scorcha IN PUBLIC like that?

Anyone could have seen them – and someone
did. Septicaemia exploded out of the house like a
nasty sneeze (probably one to go with the cold sore).

'You floozy! Shame on you!'

Trendia turned towards Septicaemia, saw
Maddasbananus, turned very red, burst into
tears, dashed back into her home and slammed
the door so hard a crow perched on the porch fell

off. Laugh? I almost died. **Kraaarrk!**

Septicaemia went straight to her neighbour to tell her what had happened and within a few minutes the whole street knew. Oh dear. Humans. What are they like? Humans, that's what they're like. Very silly, small-minded, gossipy humans.

Meanwhile, Scorcha stood there, hands on his hips, grinning at everyone, including Maddasbananus, who really couldn't stand that and went rushing off to his apartment and shut the door too, taking his weaving machine with him, so I still didn't know how it worked.

Scorcha wandered over to me and looked back at Maddasbananus's place. 'What's wrong with him?' he asked.

I shook my beak. I didn't know what to say.

Whaddya mean, that's a first? Listen, if I stopped talking, you wouldn't know anything, would you? You'd be in the dark. What I mean to say is that it's none of my business what goes on with Trendia. Her husband was a soldier, but he was in a battle and got a sword stuck in him, which wasn't very good for his health. So now she's on her own and if she likes Scorcha that's up to her, isn't it? I think he's a bit young for her, personally speaking, but there we go. What can you do?

Scorcha was still grinning and his eyes were shining. 'I've got my first race,' he said.

Aha! So maybe that kiss from Trendia was simply a congratulatory peck. Maybe. I would need more time to consider that.

'*Hoooweeee!*' I whistled. *Toc-toc-toc.* 'Amazin'!

Congratulations! When?'

'In a couple of days,' said Scorcha. 'And if I do well I'll be in the Green Team.'

'How did this happen?' I asked. 'Why has Jellus changed his mind about you?'

'He didn't. He got a new horse last week and took it out riding before it was properly broken in. Thinks he knows everything about horses, so it serves him right. He was riding down by the river and the horse got spooked by something and took off. Jellus fell and landed in the river.

He's got some terrible fever he picked up from the water. You know how filthy the Tiber is. Jellus is sweating it out in bed and can't race, so I'm in!'

'You'll be great,' I said, patting his shoulder with one wing. 'Here's Perilus. You'd better tell him the good news.'

It *was* good news too and it had Perilus practically squeaking with excitement.

'We'll all come and watch. It's going to be the best race ever and you're going to win!'

'That is up to Fortuna, Goddess of Luck,' said the soon-to-be charioteer. 'I shall make an offering to her at the temple tonight.'

'While you're at it you'd better pray that Jellus doesn't recover too soon,' I suggested before waddling over to see Maddasbananus.

The inventor was sitting in his inventing room, looking very glum.

'Cheer up,' I said.

'You saw, didn't you? How can I cheer up? Trendia loves Scorcha, and why shouldn't she?

He's young, handsome, dashing, successful –
well, almost successful. And look at me. I'm old.
I'm thirty-one! What have I achieved? Hardly
anything. I've no money, no home of my own.
I'm just a waste of space.'

I couldn't listen to this. Here was the man who,
a short time earlier, had been telling me I was
more than a raven. (Which I'm still puzzling over,
I have to say.) He definitely needed cheering up.

'Come on,' I said. 'Scorcha isn't that handsome.
For a start, he's got a honker even bigger than
mine.'

Whaddya mean, nothing can be bigger than
my beak? How dare you be so rude! Do I make
remarks about your conk? No, I don't. Go and
stand in the corner and stay there until I say you
can come out.

I draped a comforting wing round
Maddasbananus. He sneezed violently and quietly
removed my tickly wingtip from up his left nostril,
where it had somehow gone without me noticing.

'Listen,' I said, 'you're goin' to be a millionaire soon. Show me your latest invention, your weavin' machine. What does it do? How does it work?'

See what I was doing? I was taking his mind off his troubles. And it worked too. Am I clever? Yes, I am. Very. *Corvus maximus intelligentissimusimussimussimuss.*

Maddasbananus was already getting worked up about his latest idea.

'It's so simple I don't know why nobody thought of it before. You put a sheep in here.' He opened the door to what looked to me like a cupboard. That was because it was a cupboard. I recognized it from when it was beside his bed. But now I could see that the top was actually a lid and there were handles you could turn on each side.

'You put a sheep in here and you fix all these wooden arms with little hooks to the sheep's coat.'

Maddasbananus lifted the lid off the box so I could see inside. There were dozens of stick-like arms inside, arranged down the two longer sides of the box. Each little arm had a tiny hook on the end.

'It looks rather unpleasant,' I suggested.

'No, no. It will just tickle,' Maddasbananus insisted.

'You're goin' to tickle a sheep?'

'Of course not. It will just feel like tickling. Anyhow, you pop a sheep in the box and attach the little hooks. You close the door and put the lid down and then you turn both the handles. The handles jiggle all the hooks about madly –'

'That's the tickly bit,' I put in.

'Exactly. The hooks pull at the sheep's coat and turn it into *cloth*. Ta-da!'

'How does it turn it into *cloth*?'

'Because that's what a weaving machine does!' Maddasbananus grinned.

I studied the box carefully. 'It's all very interestin',' I told the inventor. 'Unfortunately, I do feel I should make you aware of one or two problems. One, Trendia doesn't have a sheep and neither does anyone else on the street and, two, the sheep might die laughin', havin' been tickled to death.'

The crestfallen inventor stared at his machine. 'It's not going to work, is it?'

'I doubt it.'

He slumped into a chair. 'It's really not my day. Trendia's never going to marry me because I'm useless.'

Poor Maddasbananus. He looked at me with such sad eyes I just wanted to give him a hug. So I did. And a biscuit too. **Kraaarrk!**

5. Who Wants Lumpy Milk?

There's something amiss. Krysis has got problems. He keeps disappearing from the house and he's looking worried. There's something bothering him, but he won't let on what it is. He tells Flavia he's got a big workload at the moment, but most of this so-called workload seems to take place in one or other of the local taverns. **Kraaarrk!** I know that because I use the taverns a lot myself when I'm on fly-about. That's when I head off to see what's what and where's where and who's who, if you get my meaning. Plus, people are always dropping bits of food all over the place so I can zip down and grab something tasty, like half a stuffed dormouse.

Whaddya mean, that's disgusting? There's nothing tastier than stuffed dormice and the

Romans love them. Anyhow, what did YOU have for lunch, eh? Chicken? Tuna? What's the difference? You think dormice are cute? SO ARE CHICKENS! Well, they were until you ate them, you brute. Unless you're a vegetarian, of course, and even that just means you kill vegetables instead WHICH IS EVEN WORSE. At least animals can run away. Vegetables just sit there, plonked in the earth. No chance of escape at all. Now that IS what I call CRUEL. Get over it!

Anyhow, Krysis is worried and I think it's to do with work. After all, he's a very important man. He's the big boss at the Imperial Mint.

Whaddya mean, does he make sweets? Of course he doesn't, worm-brain! The Mint is where all the money is made, and I mean that literally. It's a factory that makes money – coins, cash, ackers, dosh, dough, whatever you like to call it. Making a mint – ever heard that expression? No? Well, you have now. That's

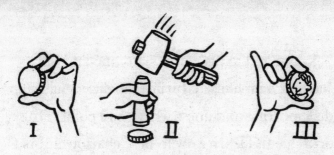

where it comes from. The Mint. Krysis is head of it. Imagine being in charge of all that doodly doodah! Shame he can't bring it home with him. *Toc-toc-toc.*

It's a big responsibility and Krysis has to report to the Emperor himself. Anyhow, he's looking well and truly haunted, as if there's a ghost in his toga just when he's trying to be in it himself.

Kraaarrk!

Just to add to his worries, his one and only son and heir, namely Perilus the daredevil, keeps disappearing and guess where he's going? To see Scorcha and learn how to be a charioteer. I bet that's giving Krysis a few grey hairs too.

Perilus is desperate to be a charioteer; either that or the god Jupiter, so he told me. There's ambition for you – he wants to be a god.

'You can't be Jupiter,' I said.

'Why not?'

'Because Jupiter is already Jupiter and he's King of the Gods. I wouldn't pick an argument with him if I were you. He's got a temper and he likes chuckin' thunderbolts around.'

Perilus pulled a face and told me I'd shattered his dreams so I told him it was better to have his dreams shattered than have his whole body blown to bits by an angry god hurling thunderbolts at him.

'Yeah, well . . .' he muttered, like eleven-year-olds do. And also when they're twelve, thirteen, fourteen, *et cetera*, *et cetera*.

(Did you spot the Latin at the end there? Well done! Go on, have a biscuit! **Kraaarrk!**)

Perilus is spending more and more time with Scorcha. Flavia just lets him get on with it. 'Boys will be boys,' she keeps saying, which is bloomin' obvious if you ask me. I mean, they can't suddenly be girls, can they? Or giraffes. But that's Flavia for you, as calm and beautiful as a fluffy white cloud in a blue, blue sky. (I really should be a poet. I could be the first raven poet in the history of the world. *Corvus poeticus romanticus*.)

Scorcha was suggesting that they should go and have some practice races out in the yard.

'But Trendia only has one goat we can borrow,' Perilus pointed out.

Scorcha raised his eyebrows several times, making Perilus laugh. 'Ah, that's true, but luckily for us Crabbus and his darling Septicaemia are out. They've gone shopping in the forum.' (*Forum* – your actual Latin again. It's like a market square, but can be used for anything.)

Scorcha ruffled Perilus's mass of floppy hair.
'So, while they're away we can pinch their goat.'

I thought I'd better put in a word or three.
'There'll be trouble,' I warned, fluffing up my
feathers for emphasis. (Feather-fluffing is very
good for that sort of thing. Take my word for it.)

Scorcha chuckled. 'Listen to the Voice of
Doom, Perilus! Are you scared, Croakbag?
Nobody will catch us because YOU, dear raven
rascal, are going to be on lookout duty.'

'Kraaarrk!'

'Don't swear,' laughed Scorcha. 'You be our
watchman and I'll give you a biscuit.'

'That's bribery,' I snapped, making my beak
clack noisily. 'How many?'

'Three.'

'Four. *Toc-toc-toc!*'

'It's a deal,' agreed Scorcha. 'Keep an eye out
for The Ghastlies. I'll get the goats and young
Perilus here can fetch the chariots and harnesses.'

They're not real chariots of course. These are small practice carts for children, but Scorcha is short and light. Charioteers have to be. (That's why that puffed-up pudding, Jellus, is such a waste of space!) The carts are made of wood and leather so they're light and fast, like the real thing.

There was a lot of bleating going on behind Crabbus's place. Scorcha may be a good charioteer, but he's hopeless at goat-rustling. Nevertheless, he soon reappeared with Trendia's white goat and Crabbus's brown one.

Perilus and Scorcha hitched up the carts and climbed in. Scorcha turned to me.

'You can start us off, Croakbag. Then hop away and watch that road for The Ghastlies.'

I raised one wing in the air and brought it down. The goats stuck out their tongues, made rude noises and they were off. Scorcha let Perilus race on ahead, watching him carefully all the time. They got to the post where there's a tight U-turn to come back. Perilus went thundering

into the corner and his cart
overturned, throwing him to the
ground, while the goat and cart went
careering ahead. Scorcha immediately
pulled up short or he might have run
over him.

'Perilus! Are you OK?'

Perilus nodded, although

he was holding his side. 'I went into the corner too fast.'

'No, no. You were fine, but lean over hard as you go into it. That keeps the weight on the inside wheel. Don't stay upright except on the straights.' He reached down and pulled Perilus to his feet. 'Try again?'

Perilus nodded. Scorcha collected the goats and walked them back to the start.

'Hey, Croakbag! Do your wing-thing again,' he called, so I did and off they went, goats blathering, wheels and hooves raising clouds of dust. Perilus was tearing along. He reached the corner. I was sure he was going to crash again, but he leaned in, like Scorcha had told him, and when he came round the other side I could see him grinning like a maniac. That's because he is a maniac! He's a real speedster, that boy; he lives for adventure and risk.

Round and round they went, with Perilus just in front. I knew Scorcha could get past him if he really wanted to, but he was letting Perilus taste victory and why not? I was so busy watching the two daredevils I almost missed seeing The Ghastlies coming down the street.

I spread my wings and swooped over the charioteers, cawing an alarm and pointing back up the road. They screeched to a halt and while

Perilus pushed the
carts away and hid
them Scorcha
led the two
overexcited
goats to their
backyards, bleating
and jumping.
Unfortunately,
Crabbus not only

heard the goats but saw them. He broke into a
run, waving his arms so much I thought he'd
take off.

'Hey! Hey! What are you doing with my goat?
I know you, Scorcha! You've been racing my goat
again, haven't you? I'll tell the magistrate. Just
you see!'

'Crabbus! Good afternoon! What a lovely day.
Are you well? You don't look well. You look –
peevish. Are you feeling peevish?' Scorcha stood
there, calmly holding both the goats by their

harnesses. One of them began nibbling the hem of Crabbus's tunic, making him even crosser.

'Peevish? Peevish? No, I'm not peevish. I'm hopping mad. I know you, Scorcha!'

'Yes, you do and I know you, Crabbus. That's probably because we're neighbours.' Scorcha smiled. My goodness, that young man was certainly keeping his cool!

'You were racing our goat!' accused Septicaemia, wrinkling her nose until it was even thinner than normal. 'All her milk will have turned into butter! It'll come out in lumps. Who wants to buy lumpy milk?'

'Crabbus, Septicaemia, how could you make such an accusation? As a matter of fact, your goat was being very naughty. She saw Trendia's goat in her backyard and decided she liked the look of her – not Trendia, of course, but her goat. She jumped over the fence to see her and Trendia's goat jumped over the fence to see your goat and if it hadn't been for me they would

have both run off to Britannia together. Luckily,
I came outside at that very moment and was
able to catch them. I was just taking them back
when you arrived and made the unfortunate but
understandable mistake of thinking I had been so
wicked as to race them. As if I would!'

Scorcha smiled and looked steadily at Crabbus,
who fumed and stamped and glared first at
Perilus and then at me. As if I might be to blame!
Me! A raven!

'**_Kraaarrk!_**' I said, raven-like.

Crabbus narrowed his eyes and carried on steaming while Septicaemia grabbed the harnesses from Scorcha and they marched off to their little house (and their one slave, who had watched the whole thing from the balcony and was silently laughing her head off). Go on, give the poor slave a biscuit! She can have one of mine.

So that was that. Not even a word of thanks from The Ghastlies for saving their goat. Do we live dangerously? Yes, we do. **Kraaarrk!**

6. One Big Secret and an Upside-down Surprise

Perilus is in big trouble with his *pater*. (*Pater*. Remember that one? Well done.) It's got nothing to do with that business with the goat and Crabbus and Septicaemia. There were guests due for dinner, in particular a VERY IMPORTANT GUEST. Krysis's boss. Have you worked it out yet? Exactly. It was supposed to be hush-hush-don't-tell-anyone-stitch-your-lips-together-top-secret, but I knew who it was because I have eyes and ears everywhere. (Mostly eyes and ears from dead animals I've stashed away in my secret hidey-holes. Very tasty, hurr hurr hurr!)

Our hush-hush visitor was going to be none other than the Emperor himself! Yes! Tyrannus, in person, wearing his own feet and legs an' all.

And he was bringing his wife, Trumpetta, and his daughter, Clumpia.

So Flavia decides on a menu for the big supper and sends Flippus Floppus off to market to get all the necessaries. Basically, that means a whole pile of dormice for stuffing, an ostrich and plenty of vegetables. Perilus, who was as bored as bored as could be this morning, decides he's going to go with Flippus Floppus, to help.

'He doesn't need help, Perilus,' Flavia pointed out with a graceful twirl of her hand. 'He's a slave. That's what he's for.'

'Mater,' said Perilus. (*Mater*. Now you've got a matching pair!) 'Mater, I am so bored I shall probably die. In any case, I'm not going to carry anything. I shall just watch.'

Flavia raised one eyebrow. (She's bloomin' clever, you know. I've tried that. It's impossible! All that happens is my tail feathers go up and my toes curl.)

'As long as you do just watch,' she warned.

'On no account carry anything. That's what slaves do and I don't want the neighbours thinking you're a slave.'

So off went Perilus and Flippus Floppus and I went with them.

'What's it like being a slave?' Perilus asked Flippus.

'Hard work.'

'Do you have to be strong? I bet I'm as strong as you.'

Hurr hurr. That wouldn't be difficult. Flippus Floppus is as thin as a broom and looks like one too. If you held a broom upside down next to Flippus, you'd get a set of twins. All those bristles would be just like Flippus's hair. Mind you, brooms don't have ears like that slave's. Do they

stick out? Yes. You could catch fish with them if you took him out to sea.

Oh, don't you want to just die laughing? I do crack myself up! I should be on the stage.

'I'm stronger than you,' muttered Flippus. 'I might look stringy, but I'm made of muscle. Do you know how heavy an ostrich is? It's like carrying a small hippo.'

'I bet you I could carry all the shopping. No problem,' boasted Perilus.

'All the way back to the villa?' asked Flippus, thinking ahead with a smile.

'Of course!'

I thought that maybe I should say something. So I did. '*Ahem, ahem.*' (That was me clearing my throat and trying to get their attention, as by this time they were comparing their rather puny arm muscles.) '*Ahem.* This is not a good idea, Perilus. You heard what your mother advised. You should not appear in public, conveyin' comestibles for consumption.'

Perilus and Flippus Floppus both stopped, stared at me and then back at each other.

'Do you know what he's talking about, because I don't?' asked Flippus.

Perilus shook his head. 'Croakbag is like that sometimes. He's a blabber-beak and loves the sound of his own voice.'

Me! A blabber-beak? My use of language is beyond compare! However, I decided not to lose my tail feathers and I carried on. 'I am simply warnin' you not to be seen carryin' anythin'. You know what your mother said – no slavin'. You're the son of a very important man, not a common slave.'

'Who's going to see, Croakbag? Stop worrying. Now why don't you flap off and find yourself a dead dog to eat.' And Perilus waved a dismissive hand at me. Oh dear. The innocent ignorance of the young. They just can't see trouble coming.

I did 'flap off' as Perilus so kindly suggested, but I didn't go far. I wanted to know how this little contest would finish. Besides, I felt it my duty to keep an eye on the lad.

They got to market and Flippus Floppus headed straight for the butcher.

'Your biggest, fattest ostrich,' he said, giving the butcher a sly wink.

'Special occasion, is it?' the man asked and Flippus nodded.

'Big dinner party. Important people. Nothing but the best. You know how it is in Rome. It's all showing off really, isn't it?'

The butcher was not impressed by this familiarity I am pleased to report.

'You'd better mind your manners,' he suggested and his eyes swivelled towards Perilus.

'Oh, this one's OK. He's going to carry it all. Says he's stronger than I am. That'll be the day.'

The butcher fetched the most enormous ostrich I have ever seen. Made me feel very pleased they can't fly. I'd hate to meet one of those coming towards me in mid-air. It'd be like meeting a flapping elephant. **Kraaarrk!**

Together the butcher and Flippus loaded
Perilus with the bird. He almost vanished beneath
it. All you could see was a dead ostrich with two
thin, knobbly-kneed legs crumpling under the
weight. Worse was to come. Flippus added three
dozen dormice for stuffing, plus a mound of
vegetables.

They set off back to the villa with Flippus whistling and looking very cheerful while Perilus panted and puffed and sweated beneath that night's dinner. They had only just left the market when who should come sauntering up to them but Tyrannus – THE EMPEROR! Only of course it was Tyrannus in disguise. The Emperor was well known for dressing up as an ordinary citizen and wandering around Rome. He liked to eavesdrop on what people were saying about him.

'Ah!' he cried on spotting Flippus Floppus. 'That's a splendid ostrich your slave is carrying.'

'Yes, indeed,' nodded Flippus, dipping his head politely. He had no idea he was talking to THE EMPEROR OF ROME, poor creature. I think Flippus would have fainted on the spot if he'd known who it was.

Whaddya mean, how did I know it was Tyrannus if he was in disguise? Because I have eyes, very beady eyes, you doubting duddle-dunce. Nothing escapes my notice. I am a one-

bird secret service. Hurr hurr.
Toc-toc-toc!

'So who's carrying that
heavy load for you?' asked
Tyrannus and he rifled
through the ostrich's many
feathers until he revealed Perilus's
anxious face peering out.

'Oh! It's a young lad! Well done, slave. I guess
you're learning your work from your master here.

FALSE NOSE AND
MOUSTACHE!

Off you go then.' And he patted Perilus on the head and sauntered on.

Well now, perhaps you think that was a lucky escape. Of course it wasn't because that very same evening the hush-hush-don't-tell-anyone-stitch-your-lips-together-top-secret special guests arrived at the villa and Krysis was at the door, wearing a worried smile, as he introduced the whole family to the Emperor, Trumpetta and Clumpia.

'Clumpia is looking forward to meeting your son, Krysis,' said Tyrannus. 'They are much the same age, I believe. Who knows? They might even marry one day, ha ha ha!'

'Ha ha ha!' echoed Krysis nervously. (There's definitely something bothering that man. I've never seen him look so jittery.)

'Here's my son now. Perilus, come and meet the Emperor.'

Tyrannus immediately recognized Perilus and Perilus immediately recognized the man from the market. Oh dear. Oh dear, oh dear, oh dear. One can never say that too many times so I'll say it again. Oh dear.

The Emperor stared. He opened his mouth and shut it again. Then he opened it and shut it again. He did that five times. If you'd peered into one of his ears, you would probably even have seen the machinery of his brain (what there was of it) creaking round and round. Finally, he found some words.

'Aren't you . . .? You are, aren't you? You? Yes. You. You are.'

As I said, the Emperor found some words. Obviously, he didn't find very many of them. However, it was enough for Flavia to sweetly enquire if there was a problem.

'But surely this is one of your slaves?' declared a puzzled Tyrannus. 'I met this lad in the market this morning, carrying an ostrich, three dozen dormice and a pile of vegetables. He's a slave, surely? A common slave?' Tyrannus grinned manically, thinking the whole thing an uproarious joke. If only.

All eyes were on Perilus. My heart went out to him. Not literally, of course, otherwise I'd be dead. It's an expression.

Krysis's voice took on a flat and deathly tone, as if he'd just been sat on by an elephant.

'Is this true, Perilus?'

'I was – helping,' Perilus said in a very quiet voice. Both Trumpetta and Clumpia burst into peals and squeals of laughter.

'The silly boy was helping a slave!' chortled
Trumpetta, while Clumpia clung to her mother's
dress as if she was about to die from laughing.

'Oh, Mater, what a pinkypoo he is. I would
never, ever marry anyone as dippy-diddly as that.
Go away, slave!' Clumpia waved the chubby
fingers of one chubby hand at poor Perilus, who
had turned as red as a beetroot with sunburn.

Krysis growled, 'Perilus, GO TO YOUR
ROOM! I do not wish to see you until
tomorrow morning when you will appear in my

study, first thing. Do you understand?'

'Yes, Pater,' whispered Perilus and he crept upstairs like a one-man funeral procession.

Was that a disaster? Yes, it was. But it was going to get worse. Oh yes, because, as I have mentioned before, young Perilus is an impulsive daredevil with reckless adventures coursing through his veins. He has the bravery of the greatest gladiators. Go on, give him a biscuit. He's going to need it. **Kraaarrk!**

7. What Perilus Did Next

I wonder what you would do if you were stuck
upstairs in your room while the Emperor – yes,
the Emperor of Rome himself – was lying on
a divan in the room below, nibbling on grapes
being fed into his mush by a young slave. Would
you not want to be there? Would you not want
to see?

Whaddya mean, you're not bothered about
seeing someone eating grapes? We are talking
about THE EMPEROR OF ROME! THE
MAN WITH HALF THE WORLD AT HIS
BECK AND CALL!! RIGHT THERE IN THE
ROOM BELOW!!!

Of course Perilus wanted to see the Emperor.
Apart from anything else, he was fed up with the
great man.

'He tricked me, Croakbag!' he complained.
'Why was the Emperor wandering round the
market dressed like some peasant? I thought
emperors wore gold and jewels and crowns.
People say that even the Emperor's pants
are gold.'

And Perilus gave me such a look, as if his entire
world had been shown up as a mirage, a folly, a
world of make-believe – which of course it was
and still is in many ways. But let us not wander
into the world of jaded philosophy and cynicism
that is otherwise known as 'being grown-up'.

I draped one wing round Perilus, this time
avoiding the nostrils. 'Perilus, I'm afraid I must

disillusion you. The Emperor does not wear golden pants. First, it would be impossible to walk in them and, second, gold is so heavy his pants would constantly fall down round his ankles so, all in all, not a good idea.'

'Huh.' That was all Perilus could find to say on the matter. 'Huh.' In any case, I could tell his mind had already moved on for his eyes were darting about the room. (It's an expression. Don't even go there.)

Perilus was considering his next move. Suddenly he got up and went across to his clothes chest. He pulled out all his togas and began tying them end to end, until he had a toga-rope. Then he knotted one end of the rope round his waist and the other to the clothes chest.

'Whaddya doin'?' I asked, rather afraid of what his answer would be.

'There is no way I'm going to miss seeing the

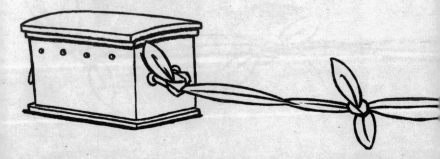

Emperor,' Perilus declared and, with that, he climbed up to his open window.

'Perilus, I do not think this is a good idea.'

'You never think anything I do is a good idea,' Perilus grumbled. 'I've had a rotten day. Why can't you say something nice for once?'

'All right, I shall. Perilus, this is not a good idea – you might fall and die.'

'That's not NICE! It's HORRIBLE!'

I shrugged. Surely it was kind of me to warn him. After all, I didn't want him dead. Where would all my biscuits come from?

'I don't want you to be hurt,' I explained. 'And fallin' from a great height on to your noddle is goin' to be rather painful.'

The daredevil fastened his blazing eyes

on me. 'I am not going to fall. I am going to see
the Emperor, Croakbag. I'll be fine. Trust me.'

I groaned. 'Trust me.' That's the last thing a
person says before they do something REALLY
STUPID. I once heard a gladiator say it just
before he went into the arena at the Colosseum
to face twenty starving lions. Needless to say, the
lions weren't starving for long and the gladiator
never came back out. Hurr hurr hurr. That's
the kind of joke that gets us ravens cackling like
crazy! *Toc-toc-toc!*

Next thing, Perilus has started to let himself
out of the window on the end of his toga-rope
and he's lowering himself down, bit by bit. That
was when the clothes chest started to move
towards the window, being pulled by Perilus's
weight at the other end of the rope.

The chest goes sliding across the floor faster

and faster and suddenly it comes up BANG!
against the wall, then gets pulled UP the wall
until it reaches the window. The lid flies open and
the rest of Perilus's clothes fall out of the chest
and rain down on him below, not to mention half
a dead squirrel I'd stashed away in there several
weeks earlier.

Perilus loses his grip on the toga-rope and
the next minute he's hanging bottom up and
swinging from side to side, looking like some

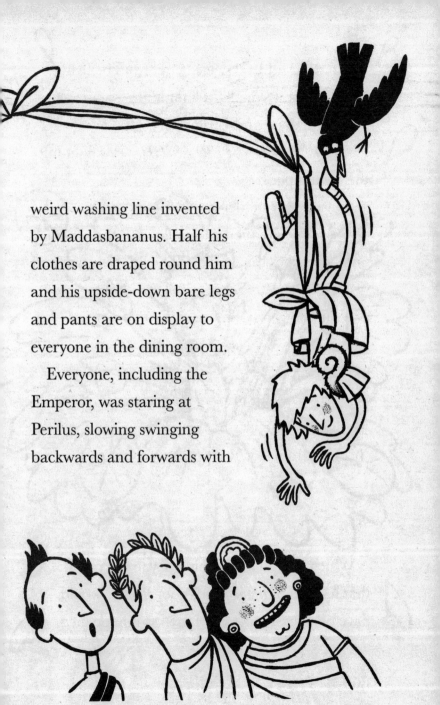

weird washing line invented
by Maddasbananus. Half his
clothes are draped round him
and his upside-down bare legs
and pants are on display to
everyone in the dining room.

Everyone, including the
Emperor, was staring at
Perilus, slowing swinging
backwards and forwards with

half a dead squirrel peering out from beneath his left armpit. Finally, a knot in the toga-rope slipped undone and Perilus fell –

PHWEEEEEEE – SPERLASSHH! – straight into the atrium pool.

Which was a Good Thing if you ask me. If that had been the ground, poor Perilus would have been well and truly hurt. As it happened, the water broke his fall and all he got was a couple of bruises, a complete soaking and a goldfish stuck in his right ear. What with that and the dead squirrel, Perilus was rapidly turning into a zoo on legs.

'It's that funny boy, Mater!' cried Clumpia. 'Oh, I do think he's such a hoot. Can we live here and make him our clown?'

While Clumpia was asking for a clown for Saturnalia, (otherwise known as the Roman Christmas), Krysis was growling orders at Flippus Floppus and Fussia, Hysteria's maid. The two slaves hurried out to the pool, bundled up Perilus between them and hastily took him back to his bedroom. The togas were removed and Perilus was left locked in his room.

Flippus Floppus whispered to him quickly as he left, 'I'll get some food to you later, master, don't you worry. I'm glad you're all right. Just stay put for now and please don't try anything else.'

I was touched. A mere slave was expressing

concern for my floppy-haired friend and I could not help but have a word with Flippus myself. 'Flippus,' I said. 'You are a good, kind man. Thank you for lookin' after Perilus and, when you bring him some food, do you think you could also manage a few biscuits? Thank you very much. **Kraaarrk!**'

8. The Beak Squeaks

Poor Perilus. It's tough being eleven. I should know. I'm only twelve myself. Of course, in human years, that's about – well, a bit more. So, moving on swiftly, hurr hurr, poor Perilus. First of all he's been mistaken for a slave by the Emperor of Rome no less and then he falls out of the sky, goes swimming in the atrium pool and completely ruins Pater's dinner party.

Now he's in Krysis's study and he's getting such a telling-off. The study door was firmly shut and I could hear Krysis working himself up into a rage, but I couldn't make out EXACTLY what he was saying. That was a trifle annoying so I padded over to the study door and leaned my feathered earhole against it.

'But, Pater, how was I to know the peasant was

the Emperor? That's cheating!' wailed Perilus.

'You know perfectly well that you never, ever pretend to be a slave. It's so – common!'

'But the Emperor can pretend to be a peasant!' Perilus shouted back, which was pretty brave of him.

'It's different for an Emperor, Perilus. Emperors can do anything they like! Besides, you are my son. I have friends in high places. If they knew you'd been pretending to be a slave, I'd never live it down!'

Ah, I thought, nodding my beak, friends in high places, eh? I'm only a lowly raven and I've got lots of friends in high places. Trees mostly. **Kraaarrk!** There's another one. What a cracker! But back to the door – or rather ear to the door.

'You behaved abominably, Perilus. And at dinner too! What on earth were you doing? Hanging upside down from your window, looking like some awful bit of roadkill that wretched raven of yours might have brought in. It was hideous.'

Hmmm. What was he going on about? Roadkill? I'd been saving that squirrel for weeks, if you don't mind. And it was VERY tasty, thank you very much!

'I only wanted to see the Emperor,' I heard Perilus mutter.

By this time, I could hear Krysis pacing up and down the room and I really wanted to find out what was going on so I poked my beak beneath the door, trying to see what was happening.

Now then, things I must tell you. Us birds have very clever necks that can twist in all directions. In fact, we can turn our heads upside down, which is very useful when you're trying to see beneath something low down, like the bottom of a door. However, I have to admit that my honker is on the larger side of big and unfortunately it got wedged beneath it. Uh! Ee! Oooh! I tugged and tugged, but I couldn't get free. I'd been trapped by my own beak! This was insane, not to mention embarrassing.

At this point, I was upside down with my claws planted firmly against the door above me and my wings flapping about uselessly like bits of old wrapping paper, and me tugging away and making muffled squeaks and squawks.

'Go to your room!' Krysis bellowed at Perilus. 'I don't want to set eyes on you all day. And next time I bring an emperor into this house you'd

better not behave like that again or you'll be out on the street with no home at all. Go on! Get to your room!'

I heard Perilus padding my way. HELP! Any moment now he'd try and open the door and there's me with my hooter still jammed under it. I'd be scraped to bits, dragged beyond deadness. All-powerful Diana, Goddess of All Creatures, save me!

ERRRRRKKKKKK!

The door was yanked inwards.

'*Aaaarrrgh!* My deak!'

'Croakbag?' Perilus stared down at me as I struggled to my feet. Ungainly. That's the word for it. I was completely lopsided owing to my neck having been twerked and twisted beyond neckability.

'My deak!' I repeated.

'Your – deak?'

'Yed! My deak!' It wasn't my fault I couldn't speak properly. It felt as if my hooter had been squeezed until the top bit had got stuck to the bottom bit and I could barely move it at all.

'Get that blasted raven out of my office!' yelled Krysis.

'I think he's hurt his deak, Pater.'

'Jupiter! Save me from this madhouse!' Krysis yelled, but more worryingly he was now eyeing me with increasing suspicion. He was trying to work out how this situation had come about.

You know that awful feeling you have in your stomach when you think you're about to be found out? That's what I had. Rumblings below.

'Croakbag,' Krysis began. 'Were you listening at the door?'

I pulled my wings together, gave my feathers a quick preen and slowly raised my head until I was peering at Krysis with one bright and beady eye.

'No,' I said. It wasn't a very good 'no'. It came out as a sort of half-croak, half-squeak – what you might call a squoak.

Krysis frowned. 'So what were you doing down

on the ground with your beak stuck under the door?'

'Peckin',' I said. Aha! See, I was going to talk my way out of this one. I'm not just clever, I AM SUPER-RAVEN! My beak was beginning to loosen up at last.

'Yes,' I went on. 'I was peckin', for food. I was

walkin' this way and just happened to be strollin' past when I spotted some escaped crumbs of the biscuit variety, to which I am quite partial, as you well know. So I bent down and started peckin', followin' the trail of crumbs as it were, and the next thing I knew my beak was stuck beneath the door and Perilus opened it, freein' my beak, and for that I thank you both. And now, if you don't mind, I shall go and wash all this floor dust off my feathers. Good mornin'.'

How do you like that then? I just walked away, a free raven, as innocent as a raven could be, which is not a lot. Am I clever or am I clever or am I SUPER-RAVEN? **Kraaaaarrrkkk!** Go on, give us a biscuit!

Anyhow, it left Perilus in a bit of a pickle. Krysis seems determined to keep the boy shut away in his room, staring across the road. As was big sis Hysteria. You know why she was staring, don't you? Scorcha was out in the courtyard, sorting all his charioteer bits and pieces and

getting ready for
his big chance
to race with the
Green Team.
Hysteria's heart
was full of dreamy
love for the young
charioteer. Ah! Sweet!

And, of course, it's Perilus's
dream too and I don't mean
he wants to marry Scorcha,
but he does want to be a
charioteer. Well, we all
have our dreams, don't we? Mine are mostly
about biscuits and sitting down.

Whaddya mean, birds can't sit down? That's
exactly the point! You humans can't fly, no matter
how much you flap your puny little featherless
arms, but flying is what you often dream about.
Unlike you lot, birds can't sit down, so that's what
we dream about: sitting around in armchairs.

Anyhow, Perilus wants to be a charioteer and you'd think there was nothing wrong with that. But Krysis? Oh no, being a charioteer isn't good enough for Pater. Pater's got his dreams. Krysis sees his son following in his footsteps and becoming boss of the Imperial Mint like him.

It's a very important, high-up job. That's why he's got such a big villa and so many slaves. But there's a problem, see? People in high-up jobs mostly like to be with other people in high-up jobs. When you're one of the high-ups, you start feeling special, like you're above everyone else 'cos they're not as high-up as you are.

I'll tell you what, though, none of you humans can get up as high as me because I can fly! **Kraaarrk!** Ah, I crack myself up. I am just SO clever sometimes. *Corvus brainus giganticus* – that's me!

Anyhow, charioteers are definitely NOT high-ups, even though some of them earn fantastic amounts of money. You ask Krysis and he will tell you that more than half the charioteers here in Rome are actually slaves, or used to be slaves until they were freed. Definitely NOT high-ups.

Now Krysis – he's not a bad dad and he's not a bad man either. He looks after his slaves. He always frees them after they've been with him for ten years, and some of them choose to carry on working for him. Maddasbananus, across the road – he used to be one of Krysis's slaves. Krysis helps his slaves get educated and find good jobs. But that's as far as it goes. They'll always be slaves as far as Krysis is concerned.

Do you think high-up Krysis wants his son Perilus to become a charioteer? Big NO-NO. But Perilus is only eleven and boys will be boys, so perhaps he'll grow out of his dream. On the other hand (or should I say 'the other wing'?), I haven't grown out of mine. I still dream about sitting in an armchair. **Kraaarrk!** Get over it!

9. Life Starts Throwing Stuff

But life goes on. That's a saying we ravens have: 'Life goes on.' We're stoical creatures, see?

Whaddya mean, you don't see at all? Oh, you don't know what 'stoical' means, do you? Like I said before, GO TO SCHOOL! But back to being stoical. It means, quite simply, that we take things as they come – the good, the bad and the in-between. Life tends to throw things at you sometimes and it doesn't always throw things that are nice. Sometimes it throws young lads into pools and sticks goldfish in their ears. **Kraaarrk!** *Toc-toc-toc.*

Anyhow, today I was having a lovely time going through one of my hidey-holes. Us ravens are always stashing our stuff away somewhere. I've got hiding places all over the place: under rugs,

behind chests and so on. So, I was
enjoying myself no end, putting
stuff in, taking stuff out,
putting it back in again. I
even found a small lump of
dead rat stashed away. That
was a tasty surprise. So there I
was, up on the roof chewing away on
the old rodent when I spotted what looked like a
ghost with itching powder down the back of its
neck hiccuping across the road at high speed and
heading for the house opposite.

I hastily rammed what was
left of the rat under a roof
tile and floated across the
road myself.

'Your *pater* won't be
very pleased,' I told
the ghost.

The ghost threw
back his sheet angrily.

'How did you know it was me?' Perilus asked.

I sighed. Sometimes it's not much fun being as wise and world-weary as me. 'I could just tell,' I told him. 'It's the way you walk.'

'I've got to help Scorcha,' Perilus declared. 'It's his big day tomorrow. He's going to race and I've got to help him prepare. He's got some new way of practising.'

'I see. Does that mean you'll be borrowin' Crabbus's goat again? Is that sensible?'

'They're out. I saw them go. Scorcha is getting the goats already.'

That much was true. I could hear an almighty clamour of bleating and blathering going on and I hoped Crabbus and Septicaemia were well out of earshot. Then Scorcha himself appeared, grinning from ear to ear.

'I've got them!' he cried. 'Time for a final practice. Croakbag, *salve*!'

(*Salve*. 'Hello.' Try and remember. 'Goodbye' is *vale*. Aren't you coming on well?)

Scorcha grinned at me. 'How are you doing? Have you come to watch?'

'I wouldn't miss it for the world.'

'Good. I've got a great plan. Perilus, help me with these two planks. We're going to tie them across the goats.'

I studied the goats carefully. They were now joined together by two short planks lying across their backs. I tried as hard as I could, but I failed

to see how a pair of goats with two planks was going to help Scorcha win his place in the Green Team.

Scorcha tightened the ropes holding the planks in place. 'Just think, by this time tomorrow I could be a fully paid-up member of the Green Team, with a real chariot and real horses, thundering round the ring at the Circus Maximus. It would be a dream come true.'

'Indeed,' I said. 'But what is this new contraption of yours?'

'Aha! Brilliant, isn't it? You see I had this idea in the night.'

'You haven't been talkin' to Maddasbananus, have you? You do realize that some of his ideas are, well, unusual?' I suggested.

'No, no. This came to me in a dream. It's brilliant. You see chariot racing is so much about balance.'

'Balance?' I repeated, and I remembered Perilus walking on the washing line.

'Yes. The track is rough. The chariot gets thrown all over the place so what I've tried to do here is to imitate the roughness of the road.'

'Ah! So you're tryin' to get the goats to throw you all over the place?' Light was dawning in my brain, like the sun rising from the obscuring mist of the early morn, allowing its radiant beams to burst forth upon the world. Oh, I really should be a poet.

'Exactly, and I must keep my balance while standing on these planks. That's the trick of it. If I can stay on my feet while these giddy goats do their best to throw me to the ground, then riding a proper racing chariot will be easy.'

Perilus grinned at me. 'Isn't Scorcha brilliant!'

Hmmm. I can't say I was completely convinced about Scorcha's brilliance or the goat-balancing idea, but one thing was quite obvious: Scorcha was going to go for it and go for it he did.

I have never seen so much dust. Scorcha and the goats set off at breakneck speed, with the

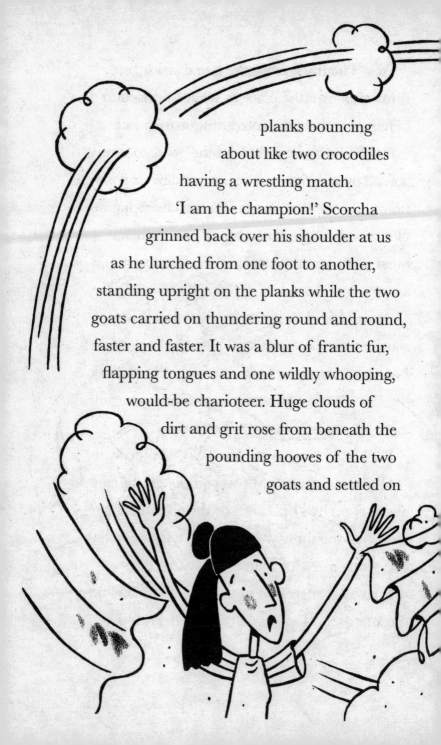

planks bouncing
about like two crocodiles
having a wrestling match.
'I am the champion!' Scorcha
grinned back over his shoulder at us
as he lurched from one foot to another,
standing upright on the planks while the two
goats carried on thundering round and round,
faster and faster. It was a blur of frantic fur,
flapping tongues and one wildly whooping,
would-be charioteer. Huge clouds of
dirt and grit rose from beneath the
pounding hooves of the two
goats and settled on

all the washing that had just been hung
out to dry by The Ghastlies' slave, Putuponn.

The poor girl screamed with dismay.

'NOOOOOO! MY WASHING!'

She came tearing out to try and rescue it
all and ran right across the path of Scorcha's
thundering plank-tank. He yelled in horror,
swerved violently to avoid
her and just missed
the terrified girl.

Unfortunately, Scorcha was now heading straight for The Ghastlies' home at high goat-speed, with no time to stop. He plunged headlong through the front door that had been left half open by the slave. I covered my ears.

KERRUNCH! BANGG!

The door came off its splintered hinges.

SKRUNNKK!! OW! THUDDD!! OUCH! OOH! SPLANNGG!

Assorted bits of broken furniture came tumbling out through the door and into the yard. Just as the dust began to settle, who should come yelling into the yard, waving their arms as if it was the end of world?

Crabbus and Septicaemia, The Ghastlies
themselves.

Poor Scorcha. There was no escape this time.
Crabbus found the young charioteer half buried
beneath a broken table, two chairs and a pile of
smashed pottery, including the olive jar. Scorcha
had olives and olive oil plastered all over his head
and chest. Meanwhile, Trendia's white goat,
quite unharmed by it all, was busily
eating Septicaemia's best rug.

Crabbus's eyes narrowed to tiny slits and a joyless smile spread across his thin lips. 'This time you're for it, Scorcha. It's the magistrate for you and then JAIL.'

Oh dear and, as I keep saying, life throws things at you, sometimes quite literally. First it was a weaving machine. Then it was an upside-down Perilus. Now it was two goats, two planks, a charioteer and a jug-load of olives. **Kraaarrk!** Nice one, Scorcha!

10. Just Big Goats!

The yard over the road was empty and silent apart from the odd bellow from Crabbus as he yelled at Putuponn. It seemed impossible for him to ask the poor girl to do anything without roaring at her.

'FETCH THE WATER!'

'IT'S TOO HOT!'

'IT'S TOO COLD!'

'TELL THAT STUPID BIRD TO STOP STARING AT ME!'

'THAT BIRD'S JUST DROPPED A DOO-DOO ON MY HEAD!'

'DON'T YOU DARE LAUGH AT ME, GIRL! GET ME A RAG!'

Oh dear, did I drop a doo-doo? Would I drop a doo-doo? Of course I would! Give us a biscuit. Give us fifty biscuits! **Kraaarrk!** *Toc-toc-toc-toc*.

But *tempus fugit* and it was almost time for the chariot racing. (*Tempus fugit* – yes, indeed, it's the old Latin again and it simply means 'Time flies', and so do ravens. *Corvus fugit*, hurr hurr.)

This was Scorcha's BIG DAY and he was nowhere to be seen. Where was the lad? I was just preening my primaries (that is to say the long feathers on the ends of my wings) when I heard a terrible screeching sound approaching fast. Was it the emergency Rome fire brigade dashing to a conflagration on all six legs, that is to say three men pulling a hose and water cart? Was it Hysteria perhaps, I hear you ask?

Whaddya mean, you didn't ask? It doesn't matter, my question was rhetorical and, if you don't know what that means, you know where you can go, don't you? TO THE DICTIONARY!

Hurr hurr hurr. Nice one, Croakbag, even if I say so myself. Which I do.

So, no firemen and no Hysteria. You'll never guess – it was Perilus! The boy daredevil himself! The boy who chases Scorcha round and round at breakneck speed and at great threat to his life. The boy who likes to hang upside down from his bedroom window. There he was, rushing towards me IN TEARS! Great gushing floods of them. Cascades! Torrents! Entire waterfalls!

'SCORCHA'S BEEN PUT IN JAIL!' sobbed Perilus. 'It's the day of his race, his big chance, and Crabbus has had him taken to JAIL!' He threw himself in a blubbering heap on the ground at my feet.

My eyes narrowed. Those wretched Ghastlies! They must have been to the magistrate and told him about Scorcha smashing up their home. I gazed down at the trembling young lad at my feet and considered the situation. It was deeply troubling. This called for the biggest, brightest, best brain in Rome. In other words, *CORVUS BRAINUS GIGANTICUS*! And in other, other words – me!

There are many things a raven can do. I can soar like an eagle in the brilliant blue azure of a Roman sky. I can turn my head upside down and get my hooter jammed under a door. I can scratch my head with one claw. (Go on, you try and do that, hurr hurr.) I can talk, even better than you sometimes. But sadly I cannot get people out of jail, nor do I know of anyone who can, certainly not quickly enough for Scorcha to make his race. Therefore, *ipso facto*, we had a problem. (*Ipso facto*. It's actual Latin again. It sort of means 'by the fact', though it's easier to think of it as meaning 'therefore'.)

Whaddya mean, I've already used 'therefore' once and *ergo* I can't say it twice? Whaddya mean, I'm saying 'therefore, therefore?' Listen, who's telling this story? I am, that's who. So I'd be most pleased if YOU STUCK YOUR HEAD IN THE BREAD OVEN! Thank you.

Toasted togas! You try to educate someone and all they can do is pick holes. Get over it!

Ahem. I shall continue. I looked down upon the sobbing creature and, wonder of wonders, a little thought began to grow in my feathery, black-as-black noddle. The brain is a wonderful thing and mine, of course, is particularly wonderful and intricate in its performance.

'Perilus,' I said, 'I do believe you have given me an idea.'

Perilus shot upright and wiped his eyes with his fists. 'You're going to save Scorcha?'

'No,' I croaked. 'You're goin' to save Scorcha.'

'Me? But how? I'm eleven. I'm only a boy.'

'Perilus, you are a boy with a man's heart – a man's heart for adventure,' I told him. 'What is more, you are a boy who is tall for his age, almost as tall as Scorcha. Not only that, you are a would-be charioteer, a boy who can handle a chariot at high speed, almost as well as Scorcha.'

I stopped clacking, cocked my head on one side and fixed Perilus with one beady, glittering, INTELLIGENT eye.

His mouth fell open. His eyes widened. 'You want me to take Scorcha's place in the race?' he whispered. 'But I could never – horses! Horses, Croakbag! I've never driven horses! And, and, and they'd see I'm not Scorcha. One look at my face! No. No, it's no good, I can't do it – it won't work!'

'In that case, all is lost,' I declared, rather

philosophically I felt. 'Scorcha won't race
and he'll never get his place with the Greens.
Unless –' I began and Perilus lifted his head
hopefully – 'unless you just so happen to be
wearin' all Scorcha's charioteerin' gear, which
is still hangin' up in his room. Your head will be
mostly hidden by his helmet. Keep your chin
down and nobody will realize you're not Scorcha,
the greatest charioteer ever.'

Perilus was definitely feeling the weight of
destiny now because he was holding his own head
in his hands. 'The horses!' he repeated over and
over again.

I sighed. 'Just think of the horses as large
goats. Very large goats. That's all you have to
do! They're horses. They like gallopin' about.
They won't even notice you're not Scorcha.
I mean, horses are not bright creatures, not like
us ravens.'

Perilus got to his feet. He clenched his fists
at his sides and stared back at me with grim

determination written right across his face.
(Not literally, obviously. It's just an expression.)

'Right!' he declared. 'I'll do it! I'll take
Scorcha's place and I'll win the race! They're just
big goats, aren't they, Croakbag?'

'Yeah,' I nodded. 'Horses! Easy-peasy. Just big
goats. Go for it, my son – and may this biscuit go
with you. **Kraaarrk!**'

11. Wedding Presents?

The villa had become rather gloomy that morning. Outside, people were rushing past on their way to the Circus Maximus for the races. They were chatting and yelling at each other.

'Up the Blues! Blues are best!'

'You've got to be joking. Blues don't have a clue! Yellows are the fellows!'

And so on. But everyone in the villa now knew that Scorcha was in prison, thanks to The Ghastlies, Crabbus and Septicaemia. Perilus was a nervous wreck, trying to big himself up for his Scorcha impersonation. Krysis was

going round banging his fists against his skull as
if some dreadful problem was coiling itself round
him like a monstrous python. As for Flavia and
Hysteria, they were clutching at each other and
sobbing wildly over Scorcha's fate.

'I shall never see him again!' Hysteria wailed.
'I shall wither away and die from a broken heart!'

And so on. Die from a broken heart? Unlikely,
I thought. She'd drown in her own tears first.

I was about to point this out when I happened

to notice Maddasbananus across the road. I was, in fact, at that moment very busy at my morning preening and had my head stuffed halfway up my left wingpit – that's armpit to you humans. I just caught sight of Maddasbananus as he went across the yard towards Trendia's house, dragging some strange bit of wooden machinery with him. This definitely required investigation, so I flapped over to see what was going on.

'It's my latest invention,' Maddasbananus said, his face wreathed in smiles. 'I've made it for Trendia. It's a sewing machine.'

'Really? A sewing machine? What does that do?'

'It sews,' Maddasbananus told me.

Hmmm. I fixed the inventor with my most glittering, piercing eye (that's the left one, by the way) and told him that somehow I had already managed to work that bit out since the clue was in the name. *Ergo*, I required to know more.

'Oh,' he said. 'Well, at the moment Trendia

does all her stitching by hand. It takes a long time. This machine will stitch things faster – twenty times faster. The cloth goes in here. The thread passes through this needle. Trendia turns this handle and the needle goes up and down, putting the thread in the material. It's my brilliant idea and it's going to make me a fortune. But now I'm giving it to Trendia and she will be so impressed she'll fall madly in love with me and we'll get married and live happily ever after while I make sewing machines for the rest of the world.'

Of course! I should have worked it out before. Maddasbananus was probably the only person, apart from The Ghastlies, who liked the idea of Scorcha going to jail, because if Scorcha was in jail he wouldn't be a rival for Trendia's attention. I couldn't blame Maddasbananus for taking advantage of Scorcha not being there. I would have done the same myself. Hurr hurr hurr!

However, I wanted to see what Trendia would

do with this amazing machine so I went along with the inventor.

Trendia answered her door, looking both shocked and worried. 'They've put Scorcha in jail,' she told us breathlessly.

'Yes,' began Maddasbananus, rather too excitedly, 'but I've brought you a sewing machine.'

'Poor Scorcha. Do you think he's all right?' Trendia wasn't even looking at Maddasbananus.

'It makes clothes much more quickly,' persisted the desperate inventor, with rather less excitement.

'What will he have to eat in jail? Has anyone taken some food for him?' Trendia wrung her hands. 'Perhaps I could stuff a dormouse for him. Do you think he likes stuffed dormice?'

'It's a sewing machine,' Maddasbananus repeated, and excitement had now turned into desperation. 'It sews. It will help you. I made it for you.'

'I don't think they have any washing facilities in jail. Poor Scorcha. He'll start getting smelly if he doesn't wash. I'll stuff a dormouse and take some soap as well.'

Maddasbananus perked up. 'Actually, we haven't invented soap yet,' he pointed out.

At last Trendia looked at Maddasbananus and I was astonished. Trendia began to BLUSH.

Oho, I thought, there is more to this than I realized. I'm beginning to think that maybe Trendia likes Maddasbananus. She's just so shy she doesn't know what to do about it. Ah! Poor things! *Toc-toc-toc*.

I wondered if there was anything I could do to help and for a moment I considered giving both of them some biscuits I had stashed away or a bit of my dead squirrel to share, but in the end I decided it wasn't appropriate. Wedding presents could come later.

Now that he had Trendia's attention, Maddasbananus began explaining his wonderful invention to her all over again. Her eyes lit up at last. 'For me?' she exclaimed.

It was Maddasbananus's turn to blush and he did – like a bloomin' rose. Sweet! He pulled the machine into Trendia's house and showed her how to thread the needle and where to put the dress she was making.

'It will get it done in no time!' Maddasbananus

declared proudly. 'Just turn the handle, slowly at first, then faster.'

Trendia did as she was told and soon the dress was whizzing through the machine and the needle was going up and down so fast my eyes couldn't watch it any longer. Amazing!

There it was. The dress was finished, stitched in a flash.

'It's brilliant!' declared Trendia, jumping up and planting a kiss on Maddasbananus's surprised and delighted cheek. She pulled the new dress from the machine, held it up and, oh dear, the whole thing fell apart.

'Hmmm,' I muttered. 'I'm not sure anyone would want to wear that.'

Maddasbananus's face turned as white as a toga. 'NO! WHY? WHY?'

Trendia was looking at the two pieces of material. 'There's only stitching on one side,' she said, giving the inventor a quizzical glance.

'So? I don't understand,' Maddasbananus answered.

Trendia giggled. 'You don't know much about sewing, do you? You have to have stitching on both sides otherwise the thread comes out. The thread goes through the material, turns round and comes back out from another hole. Your machine puts the thread in the material and then takes it straight out again so it doesn't stay in there and hold everything together.'

Maddasbananus was blushing again, but this time it was because he was so embarrassed, poor man. Once again, his invention had failed and he'd let himself down.

Trendia laid a hand on his arm. 'It's all right,' she said softly. 'It was a lovely idea and so kind of you to make it for me.'

'I'm such an IDIOT!' Maddasbananus gave the sewing machine a mighty kick. 'OW!' He staggered back into the yard and hopped away, back to his inventing room.

I was about to say something to Trendia about Maddasbananus being such a nice chap and quite handsome in an odd kind of way when I became aware of a lot of noise coming from my villa. So I left Trendia staring at the useless sewing machine and flapped back across the road, trying to avoid the chanting crowd heading for the Circus Maximus.

Flavia was in a panic, rushing from room to room with Fussia and Flippus Floppus trailing after her, and they were all shouting the same thing.

'Perilus!' (That was Flavia.)

'Perilus!' (That was Flippus Floppus.)

'Perilus!' (That was Fussia.)

See? I told you they were all shouting the same thing.

Whaddya mean, you knew that without being told? I AM telling you. I said it like that for effect.

Don't you know anything about storytelling?
Obviously not.

But we must hurry on because *tempus* is *fugitting*
all over the place now. (Remember that one? I
do hope so.) Perilus had completely disappeared
from the villa and only I knew where he'd gone –
and I'm NOT TELLING! Hurr, hurr! Give us a
biscuit. **Kraaarrk!**

12. Full Speed Ahead!

Of course I'm going to tell you. I just did that last bit for effect. I hope you're impressed.

I nipped back over to Trendia's place and landed on the window. Scorcha's room was empty. Completely empty, apart from the furniture. Do you get my drift? Of course you do. Scorcha was in jail but, more to the point, all his chariot-racing gear had gone missing. That was because Perilus had pinched it and gone off to the Circus to take Scorcha's place in the chariot races.

By this time, Flavia had alerted Krysis and Hysteria, and the whole family was searching fruitlessly for the boy. (I say 'fruitlessly', but I did notice that Hysteria was holding a banana. Oh, Croakbag! I am SO funny sometimes. Go on, give us a biscuit!)

I thought I'd better put them out of their misery so I floated back to the villa. I landed out in the *atrium* by the fountain, flapped and clapped my wings, cleared my throat, *uh-hurrr*, and made an announcement.

'Friends, Romans, countrymen, lend me your ears,' I said and then realized that was about something else, so I began again. In any case, I had enough ears of my own so why would I want to borrow someone else's?

'Listen up, everyone. Perilus has gone to the

Circus. He's planning to take Scorcha's place in the races.'

Flavia screamed and then fainted. '*Aaah!* No! My son! He'll be killed!' *SPLOP!* (That's her fainting.)

Krysis ran to her and yelled at Flippus Floppus, 'Fetch some water and throw it over her! Hurry!'

Flippus rushed to the kitchen, came tearing back with a big bowl, tripped over his own sandals and threw water all over Krysis.

'Not me! Flavia!' dribbled Krysis, trying to wring out bits of his toga. Fussia fetched more water and this time managed to half drown Flavia, who came to spluttering and making strange arm movements because she thought she'd fallen into a swimming pool. She struggled to her feet.

'Come, we must get to the Circus!' she cried. 'Oh, Perilus!'

So off we all went.

They were running, I was flapping. Have you ever tried running while wearing a toga, No? Neither have I, but it's very difficult and I lost count of the number of times they tripped over themselves, or trod on someone else's toga and fell over. It's a wonder we got to the Circus at all, but we did, and we were just in time to hear the announcer yell out the second race.

'And now prepare yourselves. Young Scorcha in the Green colours is racing his first ever race against three professionals. Let's see what he can do. Trumpeters, get ready!

BLA bla-BLAAAA!! went the trumpets. The white flag dropped and they were off!

You've never seen so much dust or heard such a roar from the crowd. Perilus was the last to get started. He looked terribly nervous and was going to have to make up an awful lot of ground. I know I said horses were just like goats, but these horses were, well, they were a lot more like extremely horsey horses. The other three teams were charging ahead, skidding round the first corner and heading up the straight to the second.

Perilus was hopeless. His chariot was all over the place. The horses were frothing and foaming and had no idea where they were going. Poor kid

– Scorcha's helmet was two sizes too big and kept falling down over his eyes. Poor Perilus couldn't see where he was going. He kept trying to push his helmet back and that only left him with one hand for the reins.

There was a mighty roar and groan as the Red chariot crashed out of the race, hurling the rider to the ground, where he almost got run over by the White Team.

'SHIPWRECK!' yelled the crowd.

Now Perilus was catching them up, but it was slow work and only two laps left.

Come on, Perilus! There must be something you can do!

Oh! A little idea just came into my *maximus intelligentissimus* brain. Hmmm. Why not? I thought, so I took to my wings and I was just flapping along, minding my own business, when all of a sudden – OOPS! I almost flew straight into a horse's right ear.

The horse, which belonged to the Blue Team, shook his head at me, stuck out his tongue and spat! He did! How disgusting! He spat at me! And unfortunately he was so busy doing that he didn't look where he was going and crashed into his companion horse and for a moment they all came to a dead stop. Meanwhile, the White Team went charging ahead with Perilus in hot pursuit. Two corners to go! Come on, Perilus!

As they headed into the first corner, Perilus

tried to squeeze round the
outside, but the White chariot held
its ground and sped away from him. He
yelled at his pounding pair of thundering,
sweating beasts.

'Come on, you two! I've ridden goats that
are faster than you!'

'Huh!' went the two horses, looking at
each other. 'We'll show you, you young
whippersnapper!' And they plunged ahead at
full steam and full snort, not to mention full

snot, judging by what was falling out
of their nostrils as they hammered the
ground with their flashing hooves.

The last corner and now Perilus took the
tight inside line, the most dangerous line
to take because it was where his chariot
was most likely to keel over or crash into
the other chariot. There was a dreadful
SKREEEEEK! as the chariots came together
and almost locked wheels. I closed my eyes.
I couldn't bear it. There was a roar from
the crowd. I opened them
again. Perilus

was through! He was heading for the winning post! He'd done it!

HE'D DONE IT! HE'D DONE IT! HE'D DONE IT!

Did I say he'd done it? I think I did. He had won. Actually, factually won! QE Bloomin' D! There was wild cheering all around. Everyone was chanting: 'SCORCHA! SCORCHA! SCORCHA!'

Perilus was carried shoulder high by the Green Team to the winner's platform. He looked a bit embarrassed and wouldn't take his helmet off because he knew everyone would then see he wasn't Scorcha. An awkward moment, eh? Definitely.

'Come on, lad,' said the race organizer. 'Take your helmet off.'

'I can't,' Perilus muttered. 'I've got nits.'

The organizer burst out laughing. 'The boy's got nits!' he yelled and the whole crowd cheered as if nits were the best thing ever. (Which they're

not, but they are quite nice to nibble. What I
might call a tasty titbit.) Perilus had won the
race and by doing so he had also won Scorcha
his place in the Green Team. Even Krysis, if
not actually cheering, was certainly looking a bit
more cheerful.

Meanwhile, just across the road from the Circus Maximus, in a dark and smelly jail, there was Scorcha himself, looking very puzzled. He had heard all the cheers from the Circus. He had heard his own name being chanted. Scorcha had won! But Scorcha was in jail, wasn't he? No wonder he was confused. Poor Scorcha. Go on, give him a biscuit! **Kraaarrk!**

13. An Unexpected Ending

Well, there we are. When Perilus got home, he was beaming from ear to ear. Unfortunately, neither Flavia nor Krysis was at all pleased.

'You went chariot racing!' snapped Krysis. 'You behaved just like a common slave!'

'You went chariot racing,' moaned Flavia. 'You could have been shipwrecked, killed. How could you? It was so thoughtless of you. I was out of my mind with worry.'

Perilus looked at me and pulled a face. I think he was wondering what he could say, so I said it for him.

'In fact, Perilus has been extraordinarily brave. He only went to the Circus to assist young Scorcha who, as you know, is languishin' in jail. It was Scorcha's opportunity to earn his place in the

Green Team and now Perilus has done that for him. I think Perilus deserves some respect for that at the very least. He went to look after his friend. That's what friends do. It's so much better than stabbin' them in the back like what happened to poor Caesar.'

Krysis and Flavia looked at me and then at their son.

'I suppose,' began Krysis, 'that if you look at it like that then there is something to be said for your behaviour, Perilus, but please do not disappear like that again.'

'No, Pater. I shan't.'

So all was well, wasn't it? Well, no, it wasn't
actually because Krysis waved a hand at Perilus
and Hysteria and told them both to go away
because he needed to talk to Flavia. Not in
front of the children, eh? You know what that
means, don't you? Maybe not, so I shall explain.
Once again, Krysis had that worried look, as if
he knew there was a large and ravenous bear
waiting round the corner to gobble him up, but
he didn't know which corner or when it would
pounce. Something awkward was going on.
Krysis had become very secretive of late. He'd
been wandering round for days with his head in
his hands.

(No, no, NO! NOT LITERALLY! IT'S AN
EXPRESSION. I KEEP TELLING YOU!)

Anyhow, you may remember – and I do so
hope you do – that I had seen Krysis not at work
at the Mint, but hiding out in taverns, drowning
his sorrows, whatever they were. Something had
been bothering him for a while so I decided

I would go and hide in the bush growing in the middle of the atrium pool and try to find out what it was.

Krysis brought his wife over to a bench beside the pool and made her sit down. He sat next to her.

'Flavia,' he began, very seriously. 'We have a problem, a big problem.'

'Is it Perilus?' she asked, as well she might because I could see Perilus balancing on the ridge of the villa roof, high above their heads, at that very moment, the idiot!

'No, it's not Perilus,' sighed Krysis.

'Is it Hysteria?' asked Flavia, listening to the little choking sobs coming from Hysteria's room where she was still moaning over Scorcha's imprisonment.

'No, it's not Hysteria,' Krysis answered.

'Um, is it Flippus Floppus perhaps?'

'No, it's not Flippus Floppus.'

'Is it Fussia?'

No,' growled Krysis, becoming irritated. 'It's not Fussia.'

'Is it, er, Maddasbananus over the road?'

'No.'

'Is it Trendia?'

Krysis suddenly put a hand over Flavia's mouth. 'Look, if you list everyone we know in the street, this will take hours. Just listen to me. This is serious, Flavia. We have a problem at the Imperial Mint.'

One of Flavia's eyebrows shot up. (I do so wish I could do that! My toes were curling again.) 'Oh! But surely you don't mean "we", darling?

You mean "you" have a problem. I don't work at the Mint, Krysis darling.'

'All right. I have a problem at work. We're losing money.'

'But, darling, I thought you made money. How can you lose money if you make money? It doesn't make sense.'

'No, you're right,' said Krysis, who was now looking not only worried, but irritated and confused. 'It doesn't. That's what the problem is. We are supposed to make money. But we're losing it. I've spoken with my deputy, Fibbus Biggus, and we have realized that there's only one explanation. The money is disappearing.'

Flavia's hand shot to her mouth. 'No!'

'Yes.'

'NO!'

'Yes!' repeated Krysis.

'NO! NO!'

'Flavia, if you say that once more, I shall push you in the pond.'

I decided it was time to put in an appearance before Flavia was drowned. '*Ahem, ahem,*' I croaked, poking out my handsome head. 'I was just takin' a little nap in this bit of shrubbery here when I couldn't help but overhear your conversation. I think I have the solution.'

Krysis didn't seem at all impressed by the way I had barged in on them, but Flavia was more forgiving.

'Really, Croakbag? You know the answer?'

'I think I do. I do understand that outwardly I manifest the appearance of bein' little more than a large black bird. What you cannot see is that beneath the tufty feathers all over my skull lies an extraordinary brain of immense ingenuity and cogitative power.'

'What's that supposed to mean?' Krysis grumbled.

I sighed. What was the point in trying to impress the unimpressible? So I got to the point. 'The reason money is disappearin' from the Mint is because, no doubt, someone is takin' it. There is a thief in your midst.'

Flavia's eyes grew wide and Krysis stared into his lap.

'That is what I was afraid of,' he muttered. 'It's the only answer.'

'It's the only answer,' I nodded.

Krysis wiped a hand round his chin. 'Once the Emperor hears of this, there'll be big trouble. I could lose my job, the villa, everything.'

Flavia grasped Krysis's hands in hers. 'No. That mustn't happen. We will find out who the thief is and bring him to justice.'

'Or her,' I pointed out.

'We'll get him thrown in jail!' insisted Flavia.

'Or her,' I added.

So there we are. BIT OF A PROBLEM. Scorcha has somehow managed to join the Green Team, even though he's still in jail, and there's a thief at work at the Imperial Mint. Perilus is now doing handstands on the roof ridge and Hysteria is taking a bath in her own tears. What on earth is going to happen next? I have no idea, but isn't it exciting? Go on, give us a biscuit! **Kraaarrk!**

Well, what IS going to happen next indeed?

**WATCH OUT FOR
THE NEXT INSTALMENT OF
ROMANS ON THE RAMPAGE**

COMING IN 2016

LAUGH YOUR SOCKS OFF WITH Jeremy STRONG

Jeremy Strong has written SO many books to make you laugh your socks right off. There are the Streaker books and the Famous Bottom books and the Pyjamas books and . . . PHEW!

Welcome to the JEREMY STRONG FAMILY TREE, which shows you all of Jeremy's brilliant books in one easy-to-follow-while-laughing-your-socks-off way!

MY BROTHER'S FAMOUS BOTTOM
Nicholas's baby brother, Cheese, is famous. Well, his bottom is, because he advertises Dumper disposable nappies . . .

Ask Jeremy

Of all the books you have written, which one is your favourite?

I loved writing both **KRAZY KOW SAVES THE WORLD – WELL, ALMOST** and **STUFF**, my first book for teenagers. Both these made me laugh out loud while I was writing and I was pleased with the overall result in each case. I also love writing the stories about Nicholas and his daft family – **MY DAD**, **MY MUM**, **MY BROTHER** and so on.

If you couldn't be a writer what would you be?

Well, I'd be pretty fed up for a start, because writing was the one thing I knew I wanted to do from the age of nine onward. But if I DID have to do something else, I would love to be either an accomplished pianist or an artist of some sort. Music and art have played a big part in my whole life and I would love to be involved in them in some way.

What's the best thing about writing stories?

Oh dear – so many things to say here! Getting paid for making things up is pretty high on the list! It's also something you do on your own, inside your own head – nobody can interfere with that. The only boss you have is yourself. And you are creating something that nobody else has made before you. I also love making my readers laugh and want to read more and more.

Did you ever have a nightmare teacher?
(And who was your best ever?)

My nightmare at primary school was Mrs Chappell, long since dead. I knew her secret – she was not actually human. She was a Tyrannosaurus rex in disguise. She taught me for two years when I was in Y5 and Y6, and we didn't like each other at all. My best ever was when I was in Y3 and Y4. Her name was Miss Cox, and she was the one who first encouraged me to write stories. She was brilliant. Sadly, she is long dead too.

When you were a kid you used to play kiss-chase. Did you always do the chasing or did anyone ever chase you?!

I usually did the chasing, but when I got chased, I didn't bother to run very fast! Maybe I shouldn't admit to that! We didn't play kiss-chase at school – it was usually played during holidays. If we had tried playing it at school we would have been in serious trouble. Mind you, I seemed to spend most of my time in trouble of one sort or another, so maybe it wouldn't have mattered that much.

It all started with a Scarecrow

Puffin is over seventy years old.
Sounds ancient, doesn't it? But Puffin has never been
so lively. We're always on the lookout for the next big
idea, which is how it began all those years ago.

Penguin Books was a big idea from the mind of
a man called Allen Lane, who in 1935 invented
the quality paperback and changed the world.
**And from great Penguins, great Puffins grew,
changing the face of children's books forever.**

The first four Puffin Picture Books were hatched in 1940 and the
first Puffin story book featured a man with broomstick arms called
Worzel Gummidge. In 1967 Kaye Webb, Puffin Editor, started the
Puffin Club, promising to **'make children into readers'.**
She kept that promise and over 200,000 children became devoted
Puffineers through their quarterly instalments of *Puffin Post*.

Many years from now, we hope you'll look back and
remember Puffin with a smile. **No matter what your age
or what you're into, there's a Puffin for everyone.**
The possibilities are endless, but one thing is for sure:
whether it's a picture book or a paperback, a sticker book
or a hardback, **if it's got that little Puffin
on it – it's bound to be good.**